Buddy the Blue Corgi

You Are Special

Written by Suzanna Lynn

Illustrated by Suzanna Smith

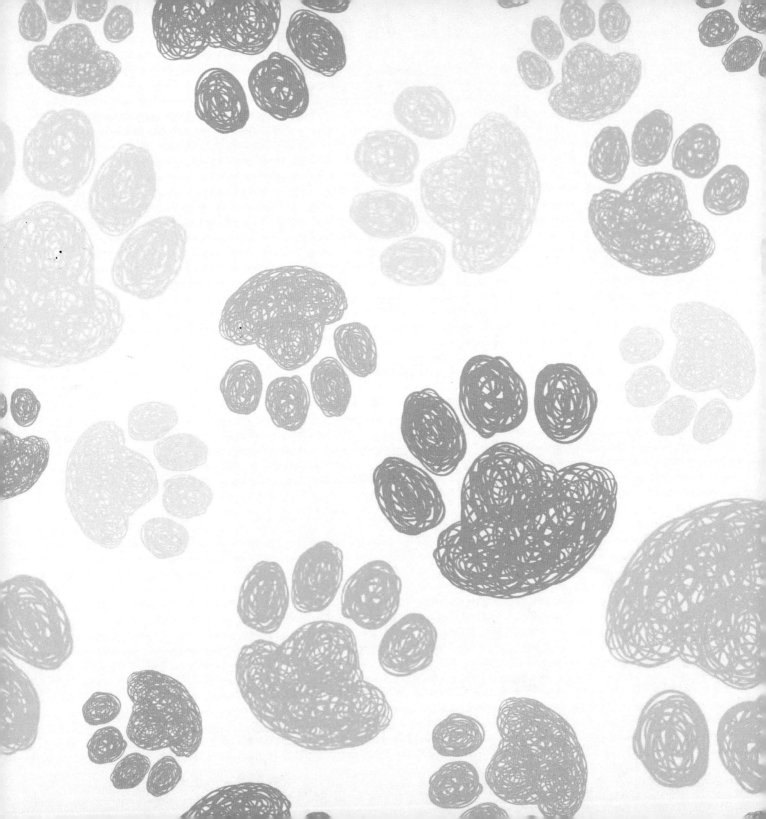

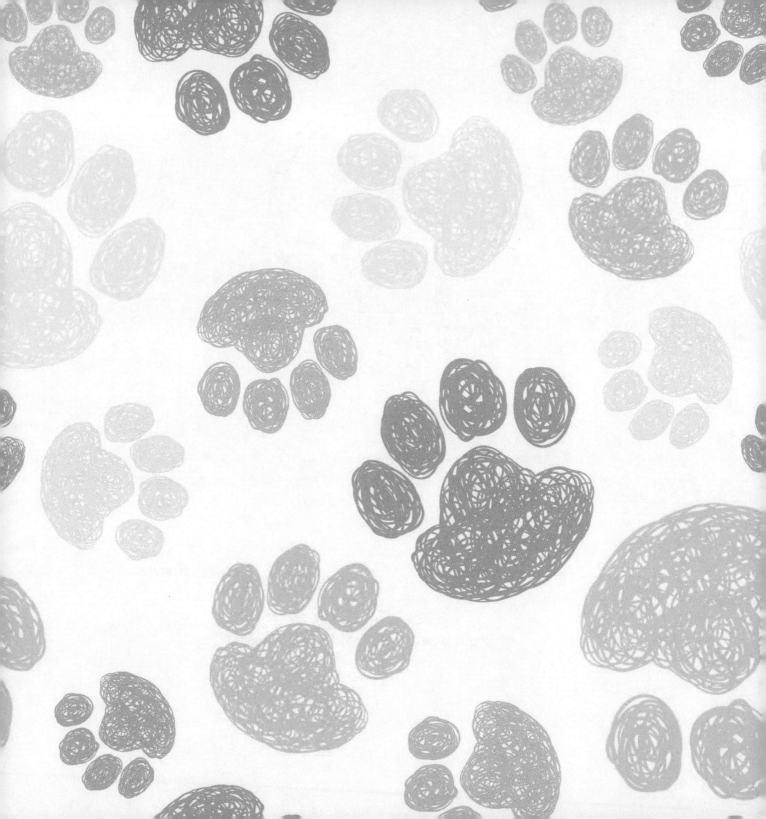

Buddy the Blue Corgi – You Are Special

Copyright © 2020 by Suzanna Lynn. All rights reserved.
Published by Lil Pumpkins Publishing, PO Box 755, Seymour, MO 65746.

Edited by Hollie the Editor
Illustration and design by Suzanna Smith

ISBN - 978-1-956079-02-9

Hi, kids! My name is Buddy, and I'm a corgi. But I'm not an ordinary corgi; I'm unique.

When someone is unique, it means they are special.

However, I didn't always feel that way. I used to think it meant I was weird.

I was born on a small farm in Kansas early one spring morning. I was one of five puppies, and our mother, Maddie, loved us very much.

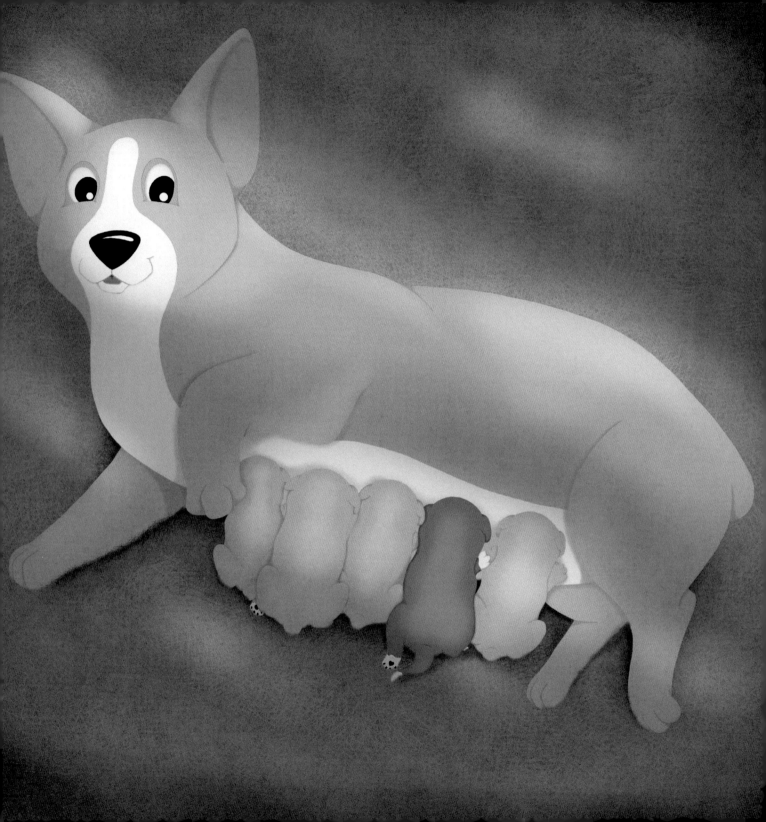

I didn't realize it at the time, but I looked very different from everyone else. After all, I was just a puppy and my eyes hadn't opened yet.

After a few weeks of snuggles and warm milk, my brothers, sisters, and I opened our eyes and were strong enough to play and explore the barn.

One day, I ran into a horse named Nelly.

"Aren't you a strange little pup?" she asked.

"What do you mean?" I asked. "I'm not strange. I'm Buddy."

She neighed with laughter. "No, silly pup, I mean you look strange. You're not like the other puppies. Their fur is tan and white. But you, you're... Well, I would say you look almost blue!"

I knew I was a little different. The other puppies didn't have long tails like me, but I didn't know the color blue was supposed to be a bad thing. Nelly's tone made it sound as bad as pig slop!

I ran to the water dish and looked down. I had the same floppy ears and long nose as my siblings, but instead of a white-and-tan face, mine was blue! I also had a big black spot over my right eye.

"I am strange!" I whimpered.

I hid in a haystack and started to cry. I began to wonder what was wrong with me.

"If I'm blue, does that mean I'm not a corgi?" I thought. "Am I even a dog?"

Momma heard me crying and dug me out of the hay.

"What's wrong my little Buddy boy?" she asked, licking my forehead.

"I'm different," I sniffed.

"What do you mean?" she asked.

I sniffed hard and said, "Nellie said I'm strange. I don't look like the other puppies. I'm blue!"

Momma nuzzled my neck. "Oh, my sweet boy! Different isn't bad at all."

"It's not?" I asked.

"No," she said. "Different just means there is something special about you. Everyone has something special about them that makes them unique."

"It does?" I asked, wondering what was strange... I mean, special about Nelly the horse.

"Of course!" she replied. "Look at Peter the pig. His tail curls tighter than all the other pigs."

"I guess," I mumbled. "But it's not the same as being a different color."

"What about the two calves, Cookie and Cream?" Momma asked. "Cookie is brown and black, while cream is completely white. But their mom was red. The whole family is different colored."

"But they're not blue," I pouted.

"What's wrong with blue?" she asked. "The sky is blue. And so are birds, and flowers, and berries too."

"Those aren't so bad." I perked up.

"I would say they are pretty special things." She smiled.

"So, being blue doesn't make me strange; it makes me special," I said.

"That's right!" Momma smiled. "Everybody has something special about them. Even Billy and Bobby—the goat twins—are each unique in their own ways."

"What about you, Momma?" I asked.
"What makes you special?"

She licked my face. "Being the momma of
a special boy like you!"

Do you feel different sometimes? Like you don't fit with others? Do you get made fun of?

Let's see what the Bible says about it.

"Before I formed you in the womb I knew you, before you were born I set you apart..." —Jeremiah 1:5

So, you see, everyone has something about them that is a little different. Yes, sometimes others can be mean and make fun of you, but remember, you are unique. God made you different, and that makes you special!

Did you enjoy this book?

If so, be sure to go leave an honest review on Amazon to let the author know!

Buddy at 8 weeks old   *Buddy's PAW-tograph!*   *Buddy at 10 years old*

Buddy the Blue Corgi lives in the deep rolling hills of southwest Missouri with his mommy, Author Suzanna Lynn.

One day while watching her children play outside with Buddy, Suzanna thought about how many lessons Buddy had learned in his life—from feeling different to learning to get along with new friends. She realized these were trials kids, including her own, go through every day.

After much prayer and planning, she began writing the Buddy the Blue Corgi stories. These stories are designed to help children understand and work through everyday problems.

Made in the USA
Monee, IL
15 September 2024

65260681R00024